Thomas Believes

John 20
for children

Dedicated to my dear children
Loren, Aaron, Rachel,
Jessica, and John.
May you, with eyes of faith,
always believe in the
risen Savior.

Illustrated by
Bill Clark

Gail Pawlitz

Copyright © 2005 Concordia Publishing House
3558 S. Jefferson Avenue, St. Louis, MO 63118-3968
1-800-325-3040 • www.cph.org

Scripture quotations are from The Holy Bible, English Standard Version, copyright © 2001 by Crossway Bibles, a division of Good News Publishers. Used by permission. All rights reserved.

This publication may be available in Braille, in large print, or on cassette tape for the visually impaired. Please allow 8 to 12 weeks for delivery. Write to the Library for the Blind, 7550 Watson Rd., St. Louis, MO 63119-4409; call 1-866-215-6852; or e-mail to blind.mission@blindmission.org.

Manufactured in Colombia
1 2 3 4 5 6 7 8 9 10   14 13 12 11 10 09 08 07 06 05

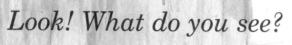

Look! What do you see?

The door is locked. The disciples are together and afraid.

Listen! What do you hear?

The disciples are talking. Some of them wonder if Jesus is really alive as Mary Magdalene said or if Jesus is dead. Other disciples wonder if the Jewish leaders who killed Jesus might try to hurt them too.

Look! What do you see?

Now Jesus is there. Although the doors were locked, He stands among the disciples.

The disciples are amazed. Jesus shows them the nail marks in His hands. Now the disciples believe that Jesus is no longer dead. He really is alive.

Listen! What do you hear?

Jesus comforts the disciples. He says, "Peace, be with you." He wants His friends to know He has risen from the dead.

Look! What do you see?

Jesus speaks special words to His disciples.
The disciples listen carefully.

Listen! What do you hear?

Jesus says that now His disciples have a new life to live for Him. He sends them out to tell others the good news that He is alive. Jesus also gives them a special Helper. He breathes His Spirit on the disciples. God's Spirit will lead the disciples to proclaim, "Jesus is alive. Your sins are forgiven."

Look! What do you see?

Someone new has come into the room. It is Thomas.
He is shaking his head.

Listen! What do you hear?

The disciples tell Thomas that Jesus was with them. They say, "We have seen the Lord! Jesus is alive!" But Thomas doubts. He wants to see Jesus with his own eyes. He wants to touch the wounds of Jesus with his own hands. Thomas says that if he sees and touches Jesus, then he will believe that He is alive.

Look! What do you see?

One week later the disciples meet again. This time Thomas is with them. They wonder what will happen this time. Soon Jesus comes again. He stands among His friends.

Listen! What do you hear?

Jesus comforts the disciples. He says,
"Peace be with you."

Look! What do you see?

Jesus walks toward Thomas. He holds out His hands so Thomas can see the places where Jesus was nailed to the cross.

Listen! What do you hear?

Jesus talks to Thomas about his doubts and fears. Now that Thomas has seen Jesus with his eyes, he believes that Jesus is alive. Now that Thomas has touched Jesus with his hands, he believes. In faith, Thomas confesses who Jesus is. He says, "My Lord and my God!"

Jesus tells the disciples that people will believe He is alive even if they don't see Him or touch His wounds. He said, "Blessed are those who have not seen and yet have believed."

Look! What do you see?

God's people are gathered in church many years later. Jesus is among them, but they can't see Him. God's people are blessed to see Him with eyes of faith. They see His grace when they hear the pastor say that their sins are forgiven. They see Him when they hear God's Word read or proclaimed. They see Him at work through Baptism. They see His body and blood given in a special way through the Sacrament of Holy Communion.

Listen! What do you hear?

The pastor speaks for God. He calls young and old to repent of their sins. He announces God's forgiveness. He proclaims the Good News. He baptizes in God's name. He distributes God's gifts in Holy Communion.

The pastor speaks for God. He says, "Peace be with you. Jesus is alive. Your sins are forgiven."

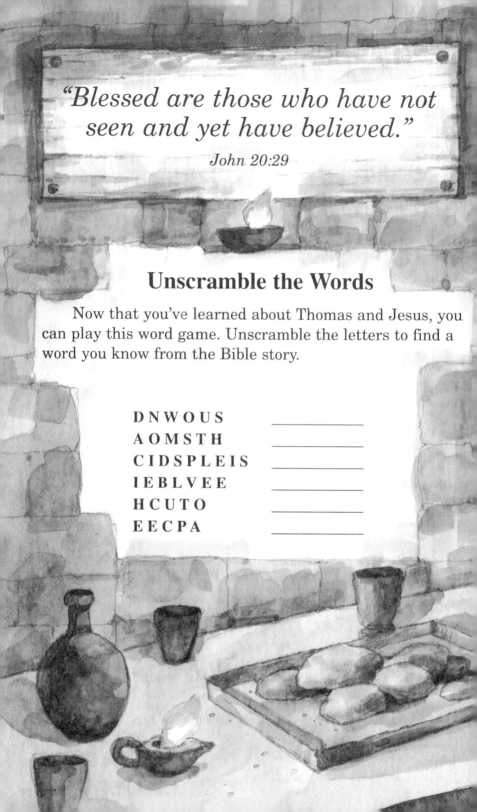

"*Blessed are those who have not seen and yet have believed.*"

John 20:29

Unscramble the Words

Now that you've learned about Thomas and Jesus, you can play this word game. Unscramble the letters to find a word you know from the Bible story.

DNWOUS   _____

AOMSTH   _____

CIDSPLEIS   _____

IEBLVEE   _____

HCUTO   _____

EECPA   _____